مفاجــأة ســميرة الســارَّة

Samira's Surprise

Written by *Nasreen Aktar*

Pictures by *Robene Dutta*
& Simon Richardson

Arabic Translation *by Sonia El Nimr*

MANTRA

يوم زيارة الجدِّ يكون دائماً يوماً خاصاً. لكنَّ اليومِ هو يومٌ خاصٌ جداً. إنَّه يوم عيد ميلاد الجد.

It was always a special day when Grandad came to visit, but today was even more special than usual. It was Grandad's birthday!

"عيد سعيد يا جدى!"، قالت سميره مبتسمة بينما بدأ حسن
يصفر لحن عيد ميلاد سعيد.

"Happy Birthday, Grandad!" Samira smiled while Hassan
played a happy birthday tune.

ركضت سميره و حسن بسرعة إلى غرفتهما بعد الإفطار ليعدا المال الذى وفراه. لكن كل ما وفراه هو دينارٌ واحد فقط.
"ماذا يمكننا أن نشترى بهذا المبلغ القليل؟" تساءل حسن.
"لنذهب للسوق، ربما نجد شيئاً مناسباً هناك," قالت سميره.

After breakfast, Samira and Hassan rushed up to their bedroom to count the money they had saved. But they only had £1.

"What can we buy for Grandad with so little money?" Hassan wondered.

"Maybe we'll find something in the market," Samira said.

نظرت سميره من النافذة
للخارج، ثمَّ سألت جدَّها،"
أرجوك يا جدي هل يمكن لنا
أن نخرج قليلاً؟"
"نعم يا جدي، دعنا نذهب
إلى السوق،" قال حسن.
إبتسم الجدُّ و هزَّ رأسه
بالإيجاب.

Samira went to the
window and looked outside.
"Please Grandad, can we go
out?" she asked.
"Yes Grandad, let's go to
the market," Hassan added.
Grandad smiled and
nodded his head.

لبس الطفلان معطفيهما
و ودعا أمهما.
لكن ماذا يمكنهما أن
يشتريا بهذا المبلغ القليل؟

So they put on their
coats and said goodbye
to Ammi. But what
could they buy with so
little money?

بحث الطفلان فى السوق عن هديةٍ مناسبةٍ. و عند كل كشكٍ
يسأل حسن سميره "هل تعتقدين أنَّه يحتاج شيئاً كهذا؟"
و عند كل كشك تقول سميره "لا."
"أنظرا هناك!" قال الجد مشيراً إلى مهرجٍ.
"يا ليته كان عيد ميلادي." فكر حسن.

At the market they looked all around for a present.
At each stall Hassan would ask, "Do you think he
wants this?"
And at each stall Samira would say: "No."
"Look at this!" said Grandad and pointed to a clown.
"Wow!" thought Hassan. "I wish it was my birthday."

بدأت سميره و حسن يحسان بالحزن، فهما لم يجدا شيئاً مناسباً للجد.

ثمَّ خطرت لسميره فكرة. قد يجدان ما يبحثان عنه في الحديقة العامة. و بينما كانا يعبران الجسر رأت سميره عن بُعد بائع بالونات.

"تعال بسرعةٍ يا حسن لنشتري بالوناً لجدي."

Samira and Hassan were feeling very sad. They couldn't see anything for Grandad. Then Samira had an idea. If they went to the park maybe they'd find something there.

As they crossed the bridge, Samira saw a balloon seller in the distance. "Quick Hassan, let's buy Grandad a balloon."

"البالونُ بدينارٍ، تعالوا و اشتروا بالوناً من هنا."

"ارجوك، هل نستطيع شراء ذلـك البالون المكتوب عليه "عيد ميلادٍ سعيد؟" سألت سميره. حمل حسـن البالون، لكنَّ سميره قالت له "أنت صغير.

"£1 a balloon!" shouted the balloon seller. "Come get your balloons here."

"Please can we have one that says Happy Birthday?" asked Samira.

Hassan took the balloon but Samira told him, "You're too young.

و قد يضيع منك البالون."
و حاولت أن تأخذه من يده.
"لن أضيعه!" قال حسن متشبثاً بالبالون.

"You'll just lose it!" and she tried to
snatch it from him.
   "I won't lose it!" said Hassan, not
letting go.

حاولت سميره أن تسحب البالون من يد حسن بعنف.

Samira pulled harder and the balloon slipped out of Hassan's hand.

و حسن يحاول منعها، و بين شدٍّ و جذبٍ
طار البالون بعيداً. وقفت سميره تنظر بحزنٍ إلى
البالون الذي بدأ يختفي خلف السَّحاب.

But Samira wasn't holding
it tightly enough and the
balloon flew away.
With horror she
watched as it
disappeared
into the
clouds.

مشت سميره و حسن مع الجدِّ في الحديقة العامة و هما يتساءلان ماذا سيفعلان فهما الآن بدون مال وبدون هديه.
و فجأة رأت سميره شيئاً. "أنظر هناك!" همست لحسن.

They walked around the park with Grandad, wondering what to do. They had no money and no present.
Suddenly Samira saw something. "Look Hassan!" she whispered.

تحت المنصَّه التي تقف عليها عادةً فرقة الموسيقى. كانتْ هناكٍ بحموعةٍ من المهرِّجين يلعبون بالكرات. و رأوا أيضاً مهرجاً يمشي على عصيٍّ خشبية، لم يروا في حياتهما أطول منه. "ربما يستطيعون مساعدتنا،" همس حسن.

There under the old bandstand was a group of clowns juggling, and the tallest stiltman they had ever seen. "Maybe they can help us," whispered Hassan.

ركضت سميره الى المهرج
الطويل وحكت له عن عيد
ميلاد الجد و كيف أضاعا
البالون.
"هل تستطيع مساعدتنا؟"
سألت.

Samira ran over to the
stiltman and told him all
about Grandad's birthday
and how they had lost the
balloon.

"Please can you help
us?" she asked.

"كيف يمكنني ان أساعدكما؟"، سأل المهرج وهو يحني ظهره كي يقترب منها.
"هل تستطيع أنت و أصدقاؤك أن تقدموا لجدي عرضاً بالكرات؟" سألت سميره.
"أرجوك .. سيكون ذلك مفاجأةً ساره له."

"How can I help?" said the stiltman bending closer.
"Would you…would you and your friends juggle for my Grandad?"
Samira asked him. "Please, it would give him such a lovely surprise."

دعا المهرج الطويل اصدقائه
المهرجين:"تعالوا.. علينا أن نقدم
عرضاً خاصاً."
مسكت سميره يد المهرج الطويل و
قادته حيث كان حسن و الجد
ينتظران.

The stiltman called to all his
friends: "Come, we have a
surprise to deliver."
    Samira took him by the hand
and led him over to where
Grandad and Hassan were
waiting.

كان الجد على وشك أن يوبخ سميره لانها إبتعدت عنه بدون إذن منه، عندما تجمعت حوله بمجموعة المهرجين.

"هل أنتَ جدُّ سميره؟" سأل المهرج الطويل.

"نعم" قال الجد.

"إذن أهلاً وسهلاً بك في عرض خاص لك. بمناسبة عيد ميلادك." و شاهَد الجدُّ بفرحٍ المهرجين وهم يتقاذفون الكرات و يغنون.

Grandad was about to tell Samira off when all the clowns came over. "Are you Samira's Grandad?" asked the stiltman.

"Yes," Grandad answered.

"Then welcome to the birthday show," said the clown.

Grandad watched with joy as the clowns juggled and sang to him.

By the end of the show others had gathered round to see what was going on.

They all sang 'Happy Birthday' to Grandad.

Then the stiltman said, "Before we go, we have one more surprise for you."

Samira and Hassan could hardly believe their eyes when one of the clowns came forward holding the lost balloon!

و عند إنتهاء العرض كان عددٌ كبيرٌ من الناس متجمعين حولهم يشاهدون المهرجين. و غنى الجميع "عيد ميلادٍ سعيدٍ" للجد. ثمَّ قال المهرج الطويل للجد: "قبل أن نذهب هناك مفاجأةٌ لم تصدق سميره و حسن أعينهما عندما تقدمت مهرجةٌ من المجموعة و بيدها البالون الضائع.

"هذا البالون هدية خاصة
من سميره و حسن لكِ"
قالت المهرجه وهي تقدم
البالون للجد.
"هذه احسن هدية عيد
ميلادٍ تلقيتها في حياتي!"
قال الجد وهو يبتسم.

"This is a special
present from Samira
and Hassan to you,"
said the clown as she
gave Grandad the
balloon.
"This is the best
birthday surprise that
I have ever had!" said
Grandad smiling.

To all those who like happy surprises - N.A.

Mantra Publishing
5 Alexandra Grove
London N12 8NU

Our thanks to Parween Akhtar & family,
Queens Park Lower School, Bedford and Daniel Sansome